Oscar's
Lonely
Christmas

Holly Webb

stripes

For Tom

STRIPES PUBLISHING
An imprint of Magi Publications
1 The Coda Centre, 189 Munster Road,
London SW6 6AW

A paperback original
First published in Great Britain in 2010

Text copyright © Holly Webb, 2010
Cover illustration copyright © Sophy Williams, 2010
Inside illustrations copyright © Katherine Kirkland, 2010

ISBN: 978-1-84715-138-4

The right of Holly Webb, Sophy Williams and Katherine
Kirkland to be identified as the author and illustrators
of this work respectively has been asserted by them in
accordance with the Copyright, Designs and Patents
Act, 1988.

A CIP catalogue record for this book is available
from the British Library.

Printed and bound in the UK.

10 9 8 7 6 5 4 3 2 1

Chapter One

Hannah took off her gloves and stuffed them in her pockets. The cold wind was stinging her cheeks, and she looked up at the sky hopefully. Perhaps it would snow soon? It was only November, but it was so cold already! She reached into the tub of winter bird food and scooped out a big helping, scattering it over the bird table.

Then she smiled to herself. She was sure she could hear some sparrows and coal tits in the winter jasmine that was growing up the fence. They were scuffling about eagerly, waiting for her to go so that they could swoop in on the delicious mealworms that were their favourite part of the mixture.

She closed the tub and put on her gloves again – it was so cold her fingers had already started to hurt. Then she crept quietly back to the garden bench and curled up in the corner. If she was very, very quiet and still, the birds might come while she was there. It would be more sensible to go inside and watch from her bedroom window, but she loved seeing the birds up close. They were so funny, the way they squabbled and shoved each other off the bird feeders. Hannah's family had five different bird feeders, and their garden was very popular with the local birds.

Hannah watched, snuggled inside her big scarf and furry hat, smiling to herself as a robin bossily sent all the other birds flapping off into the bushes. She wasn't going to be able to stay out here much longer; she could hardly feel her fingers. Hugging herself, she slipped into her favourite daydream – that she was cuddled up with a dog next to her, keeping her warm. Almost any dog would do, to be honest. She would really love a big dog that she could hug, but even a little dog would be wonderful.

Of course, as this was a daydream, she might as well have her all-time favourite. Daydream-Hannah sat there with her arms around a huge, black-and-white spotted Dalmatian. Just like Pongo from her favourite film, *101 Dalmatians*. Hannah had watched both versions over and over, and Dalmatians were her dream dogs.

Hannah's mum and dad had been thinking about getting a dog for ages – at least, they always *said*, "We'll think about it," whenever Hannah asked. Her dad was quite keen – he loved going on long walks, and he'd shown her pictures of the dog he'd had when he was a boy. But Hannah's mum was a bit anxious about Zak, Hannah's little brother. She was worried that a dog

8

wasn't a good idea with a toddler around. But Zak was coming up to three now, and Hannah had started dropping hints about dogs again. She didn't think a dog would be a problem for Zak at all – he loved animals as much as Hannah did, and whenever he met a dog he always wanted to hug it. It was more likely that the dog would need protecting from Zak than the other way around.

Just as she was thinking about her little brother, Hannah heard the kitchen door bang, and he stumbled out into the garden, calling her name.

Hannah gave a cross little sigh as Zak frightened all the birds away. She'd been enjoying the peaceful moment without him around.

But as he wobbled round the corner of the house she couldn't help smiling. Zak was wearing his big red snowsuit, and it was so stiff and padded that he could hardly move. He looked as though someone had inflated him like a balloon.

"Hannah! Hannah!" He came over and grabbed her hand. "Mummy wants you!"

Hannah's mum was coming out now too, a big scarf wrapped around her neck. "You must be frozen sitting out here for so long! Did you see any interesting birds?"

Hannah shook her head. "Only the normal ones. I was about to come in, it's getting dark."

Mum was beaming. "We came out to tell you some news! I've just had a phone call – one I wasn't expecting." She took a deep breath. "It was from the lady who runs Dashing Dalmatians."

Hannah sat bolt upright, staring wide-eyed at her mum. "Is that – is that a Dalmatian *breeder*?" she asked. "Why did she call you?"

Her mum smiled even more widely. "Because I rang her a few weeks ago, to ask if we could go on the list for one of the next litter of puppies."

Hannah sprang off the bench and threw her arms around her mum. "Really? You didn't tell me! We're going to get a Dalmatian puppy? You mean it?"

Mum nodded. "Let's go and talk about this inside, I'm freezing!"

Hannah raced into the house, tugging off her coat and scarf, and unzipping Zak from his suit. She ran to put her things away, then skidded back into the kitchen. "Please tell me!"

Her mum laughed. "I should agree to

getting a puppy more often… Yes, your dad and I decided that maybe you and Zak were old enough now for us to have a dog. Your dad wanted a big dog and you were desperate for a Dalmatian, so we found this lady – Lisa, she's called – on the internet. She lives about twenty miles away, close to Mill Green."

Hannah nodded. Mill Green was a little village she'd visited on a school trip to see the working watermill.

"She breeds Dalmatians – only two or three litters a year, so we thought we might have to wait quite a while for a puppy. But it turns out that someone who'd put her name down for one of the latest litter has changed her mind." Her mum frowned. "Something about not quite the right markings. Lisa said she'd explain it all properly when we went to see the puppy. She said it shouldn't matter at all, as we'd told her we weren't looking for a show dog."

"When can we go and see the puppy?" Hannah gasped. She hardly knew what to say, she felt so excited.

"How about tomorrow? Oooh, Hannah, don't squash me!" Her mum laughed as Hannah flung her arms around her waist. "So, you're pleased, then? You haven't changed your mind about Dalmatians?"

"Of course not!" Hannah cried. "They're the best dogs ever! We're really going to see some tomorrow?"

"Absolutely. It had to be a Saturday, so your dad can come too." Mum smiled. "He's going to get a big surprise when he gets home!"

Hannah's dad was just as excited as she was about the puppy. Mum told him all about the phone call over dinner.

"That's just such good news," he murmured. "I thought we'd have to wait ages. We wanted to make sure we got a puppy from a proper breeder, you see, Hannah. Dalmatians can be a bit nervous and excitable, and you have to be careful to meet the parent dogs, that kind of thing. Mum said the lady from Dashing Dalmatians was very nice when she phoned her. She gave her all sorts of test results and told her lots about the breed." Then he frowned and glanced over at Hannah's mum. "I've just thought. We did say we were going to try and avoid getting a puppy around Christmas though, didn't we?"

Hannah's mum nodded slowly. "Oh, goodness, I'd forgotten that. I just didn't think." She paused for a moment. "Lisa said that the puppies were six weeks old now, and we could take our puppy home at about eight weeks. So that would be the first week of December, I suppose. Oh, that *is* a bit close to Christmas."

"Why can't we get the puppy before Christmas?" Hannah asked, her voice starting to squeak with panic – they couldn't change their minds now!

Her dad rubbed her shoulder. "It's just that Mum and I said that we wouldn't ever get a dog as a Christmas present – so many puppies end up at shelters after Christmas. And it's quite a stressful time for a dog, with loads of people around, and the house all turned upside down."

"But you aren't getting us a dog for Christmas!" Hannah pointed out quickly, her heart thudding with hope. "The puppy just happens to be coming close to Christmas, that's all. It doesn't really make the puppy a Christmas present!" She dug her fingers into her hands, looking anxiously from Mum to Dad. Then she added, in case that had sounded greedy, "But I don't want anything else for Christmas, it's OK. Just maybe a dog lead?"

Dad laughed. "Don't worry, I'm not saying we can't get a puppy. I was just wondering if now was the best time. But to be honest, I'm sure getting a puppy is a big upheaval whenever you do it."

"So ... can we still go tomorrow?" Hannah whispered.

Her mum and dad exchanged a look, and smiled.

"Yes," Mum told her. "We'll go."

"Please-may-I-leave-the-table?" Hannah rattled off. "I don't want any pudding, thanks. I'm going to go and look up Dalmatians on the computer!"

Chapter Two

Hannah sat in the back of the car next to Zak, biting her lip. Mum had got sick of her asking if they were nearly there, and she'd told Hannah she'd turn the car round if she said it again. It was just that she was desperate to know!

"Look, there's a sign for Mill Green," Dad said, taking pity on her. "Not far now."

Hannah nodded, staring hopefully out of the window. Then she laughed and pointed at a sign standing in the garden of a house just ahead. "Look! It's all spotty!"

Mum put her indicator on. "That has to be it," she said. "Yes, it says Dashing Dalmatians." She parked the car in the driveway.

Hannah could hear excited barking as she got out of the car, and ran round to help Zak undo his car seat straps. "We're here, Zak! Going to see the dogs!"

"Dogs!" Zak clapped his hands excitedly.

Already, a friendly-looking woman was opening the door of the house, and beside her – Hannah caught her breath at the sight – were two big Dalmatians.

They were so beautiful, snow-white, with a dappling of glossy black spots all over.

"Dog! Dog!" Zak squeaked delightedly, jumping up and down and pulling on Hannah's hand.

The owner of the dogs laughed. "Somebody's keen, anyway. I'm Lisa. And this is Robby and Bella. They're very friendly, you can stroke them. Just watch your little brother though, won't you? The dogs are a lot bigger than he is; they might knock him over by accident."

Hannah nodded. "I'll hold his hand," she promised. "He loves dogs. We both do." She stretched out her free hand to Bella, who sniffed it interestedly and then gave her a gentle lick.

"Urrgh!" Zak giggled.

"I don't mind," Hannah sighed, and stroked Bella's soft nose and round her silky spotted ears. Bella was so gorgeous. And a dog just like Bella might be theirs soon. It was hard to believe.

"Is Bella the mum of our puppy? The puppy who might be ours, I mean," Hannah added hastily. She knew that Lisa would want to check them out before she allowed them to have one of her puppies.

Lisa smiled. "No, she's too young to have pups just yet – she's the big sister of our new puppies. Robby here is their dad, though. Their mum's called Chrissie. Do you want to see them?"

Hannah couldn't speak, she was so excited. She just nodded so hard her ponytail flew up and down.

"Come inside and let me take your coats. They're a good age to meet now," Lisa explained, as she led Hannah's family through the house, with the two Dalmatians nosing at them inquisitively.

"Six weeks old. Their spots have come through. Although they'll still get more, you can see what they're going to be like when they're older. And they're starting to really enjoy meeting people."

Hannah looked up at her mum and dad eagerly, and her dad squeezed her shoulder. "You look like you're about to meet the Queen!" he told her in a whisper.

"I feel like I am!" Hannah whispered back.

"This used to be our dining room, before we started breeding puppies!" Lisa explained, as they came to a door at the end of the hallway. "Now we use it as a puppy room." She opened the door and led them in. A wire pen occupied about half the room — and it was full of puppies. They were tumbling and squirming over each other and their mother in a black-and-white spotted mass.

"Oh, look at them!" Hannah breathed. "There are so many!"

"How many are there?" Hannah's dad asked Lisa. "I keep losing count!"

"Twelve." Lisa smiled. "It's a huge litter – the biggest we've ever had."

Hannah leaned over the wire netting to see the puppies, and Zak followed her, cooing delightedly at the beautiful little things. Chrissie, the puppies' mother, watched Hannah and Zak closely, then looked up at Lisa as if to ask if the children were safe.

"It's all right, Chrissie," Lisa said gently.

"I can't tell them apart," Hannah murmured, sitting down to get a closer look at the puppies rolling around the pen. "Oh! Except that one! He's got a patch round his tail!"

The patched puppy seemed to know he was being talked about. He pottered over to the wire, and looked at Hannah and Zak with his head on one side.

Hannah giggled at his funny little face, and the puppy jumped back in surprise.

"I'm sorry, I didn't mean to scare you," Hannah told him gently. "I only laughed because you're so sweet."

The puppy edged closer again and put out a bright pink tongue to lick Hannah's fingers – she'd been holding on to the wire without even realizing it.

"Me! Me!" Zak squeaked, making the puppy jump again. He eyed Zak suspiciously and took a step sideways, closer to Hannah. Then he leaned his head against the wire and looked up at her.

Hannah tried not to laugh and scare him again, but it was so difficult. It was almost as if the puppy was talking to her – *Scratch my ears, please.*

The puppy sighed delightedly as Hannah scratched behind his lovely white-dappled ears. This was good. The little one was a bit loud and bouncy, but this girl was doing excellent ear-scratching. He glared at one of his sisters as she came too close. The girl was his, and he had no intention of sharing. His sister trotted away, back to curl up with their mother.

"Well, he's certainly taken to you," Lisa commented. She sounded pleased, and Hannah glanced up at her hopefully. Did that mean they would be allowed to have a puppy? Maybe even – this puppy? Hannah could see that they were all gorgeous, but this one just seemed to have chosen her.

Dad had crouched down next to Hannah to look at the puppies. "Is there a particular puppy we can have?" he asked Lisa. "You mentioned something on the phone yesterday…"

Lisa nodded. "Yes. You know about our waiting list, of course. This litter have all been promised to people who've been on the list for a while.

They'll be going to their new homes over the next few weeks."

Hannah's heart seemed to fall into her stomach. So they couldn't have one of these wonderful puppies? Mum must have misunderstood somehow. She looked down at her puppy, his eyes blissfully closed as she tickled him. He was so perfect...

"But one of the ladies who wanted a puppy has changed her mind – she really wants a show dog, you see, and the puppy who was left when she came to see them yesterday won't be up to showing."

Mum looked confused. "Why not? They're all so beautiful. Can you really tell now whether they won't be show dogs?"

Hannah looked round, her eyes shining. "It's this puppy, isn't it? Please say it's this one!"

The puppy stared up at Lisa too, as though he wanted to hear the news. He wagged his little whip-like tail, with the pretty patch round the base.

"Yes." Lisa smiled at her. "How did you know?"

Hannah looked shy. She'd read so much about Dalmatians, but she was sure that Lisa knew loads more, and she didn't want to sound silly. "They aren't really supposed to have patches, are they?" she murmured. Lisa nodded encouragingly, so she went on. "The puppies are supposed to be born snow-white, and then the spots grow when they're a couple of weeks old and they keep on growing for ages – until they're about a year old even." She looked over at all the puppies. They were still mostly white, and their spots were only the size of currants. "But sometimes you get puppies born with black patches." She stroked the puppy's ears again. "But I've never seen a picture of a puppy with a patch on his tail!"

"Neither have I!" Lisa laughed. "He's really special. But he'd be no good in the show ring – they don't allow patches. So he can only ever be a pet." She reached over the wire netting, and gently picked up the puppy, and then she held him close to Hannah. "Would you like him on your lap?"

Hannah nodded. She held out her arms to cuddle the puppy, and he snuggled on to her lap. Zak sat next to her, patting the puppy on the bottom.

But Dad was looking worried. "If there's something wrong with him, maybe we ought to wait…"

"There's nothing wrong with him!" Hannah protested. Her voice was sharp with fear that Dad might say no, and the puppy's eyes widened. He whimpered, unsure what was wrong.

"Try not to speak too loudly," Lisa said, her voice soothing. "Dalmatians are quite highly-strung; you need to be very calm and gentle."

"Sorry," Hannah whispered, half to Lisa and half to the puppy.

"You're doing really well," Lisa said reassuringly. Then she looked over at Hannah's dad. "He's perfectly healthy.

You weren't planning to take him to shows, I thought?"

Hannah looked hopefully at her dad. "We just want him for a pet. And he might even be better than a normal Dalmatian," she whispered. "Sometimes they can be deaf, but ones with patches usually hear fine."

Lisa laughed in surprise. "You really have been doing your homework."

"I love Dalmatians," Hannah told her. "I've been dreaming of having one, ever since I can remember."

"Hannah's right about the deafness," Lisa explained to Hannah's mum and dad. "But Chrissie and Robby both scored well on the hearing tests, and the pups are going to be tested next week."

"I know they need lots of exercise too,

and they need to be around people. But Dad's going to take me and the puppy on long walks every day," Hannah explained. "And Mum and Zak are at home, even when I'm at school."

"That's great! Dalmatians have loads of energy, and they get bored very easily, because they're so clever. You'll need to take him to training classes. I can recommend a good trainer close to you."

"So we can have him?" Hannah asked, cuddling the puppy close, and looking anxiously between Lisa, and her mum and dad.

Lisa smiled. "I think you'd give him a lovely home. He's really settled with you, and he's been quite nervous with some of the other visitors."

Dad nodded slowly, and Hannah laid

her cheek gently against the puppy's soft head. He made a happy little cooing growl, and she giggled. "You're pleased too, aren't you, little pup?"

The puppy yawned hugely, showing his little pointy teeth, and curled up in Hannah's lap. He looked as though he wasn't going anywhere.

Mum reached down to stroke him. "I don't think it's up to us at all. He's definitely chosen you, Hannah!"

Chapter Three

"We're bringing the puppy home the weekend after next!" Hannah whispered to her best friend Lucy at school on Monday.

"You're so lucky! I wish we could have a dog, but my mum just says we don't have time to look after one properly."

"You can come on walks with us," Hannah offered.

"Oh, I think it's nearly our turn!" Lucy looked over at their teacher, Mr Byford, who was standing behind them at the back of the hall. "There's only Izzy and Ben before us."

Their class were auditioning for the school Christmas play. Hannah was hoping for a big part this year. She loved being in plays, but she always felt really nervous when they had to try out, and she'd never been given much to say before. She and Lucy had to read a scene from the play from up on the stage, so Mr Byford could hear how loudly and clearly they could speak.

"Are you nervous?" Lucy muttered. "I am!"

Hannah smiled. Lucy was a brilliant dancer and had done loads of ballet exams. She was bound to be given a part with some dancing. "You know, I'm so excited about our puppy, I actually don't feel nervous at all!" she said. Usually nerves made her tummy feel funny.

"Right, Lucy and Hannah!" Mr Byford called, looking at his list.

"Break a leg!" Hannah told Lucy, and they both crossed their fingers for luck.

Two days later, Hannah dashed out of school to tell her mum the good news.

Mum was waiting in the playground with Zak in his pushchair. "Did you get a good part?" she asked, seeing Hannah's beaming face. The girls had had to wait for Mr Byford to make up his mind. It was lucky that Hannah had been so excited about the puppy, or it would have been torture.

"I'm going to be the angel!" Hannah told Mum. "It's the main part, I do all the storytelling! And Lucy's the innkeeper's daughter. She gets to dance."

"Well done, Hannah!" Her mum gave her a hug. "You'll have to tell Gran when she comes round for tea tonight."

"Dog?" Zak asked, seeing that everyone was happy and hoping it meant more puppies.

"Oh, sweetie, not yet. Soon," Mum promised, as they headed out of the gate. Zak was just as desperate as Hannah for their puppy to come home, and he'd even taking to curling up on the lovely blue dog cushion they had bought. They'd had to do a huge shopping trip at the pet store to get everything the puppy would need.

"Only another ten days!" Hannah beamed. "And the puppy's bringing me luck already. Maybe I'm going to be an Oscar-winning actress!" She stopped dead in the middle of the pavement. "Oscar! Mum, can we call the puppy Oscar? That's such a cute name."

Mum looked at her thoughtfully. "Mmm. I like it. Definitely better than Freckles, and all those other spotty names we were thinking of."

"He looks like an Oscar," Hannah said. Oscar. Her puppy. It was only a little while longer until he came home!

Hannah carried the puppy carefully into the kitchen. "Look, this is your bed." She gently set Oscar down next to the big blue cushion. The puppy looked at it thoughtfully. It was huge, but it looked comfy. He hopped his front paws up on to the edge of the cushion, and then scrabbled to get his back paws on too. He sniffed round the cushion, interested in the smell of newness. Then he looked hopefully at Hannah. The cushion was too big for him all by himself. Would she come and snuggle up with him?

"Dog bed!" Zak squawked, pushing past Hannah and flinging himself on to the cushion with Oscar.

Oscar cowered back, horrified by this noisy thing that had nearly landed on him. Whimpering, he wriggled off the cushion, and slunk over to Hannah.

"I want do-og!" wailed Zak, and Mum picked him up.

Hannah gently scooped the puppy into her arms. "He really frightened Oscar!" she whispered crossly to Mum. She was trying hard not to sound angry, after what Lisa had told them about Dalmatians being nervous.

"Zak doesn't really understand about being gentle," Dad explained. "He'll get there."

43

Hannah sniffed. Mum and Dad never told Zak off – whenever he was naughty, they always said he was just little. Well, Oscar was littler! Hannah just hoped that Mum wouldn't let Zak upset Oscar while she was at school.

The first day with Oscar was so special. Hannah hardly left the kitchen. Oscar was going to stay in there for the first few days – with trips out into the garden for wees, of course. She had bought him a special squeaky bone with her own money, and he loved it. He kept jumping on it and shaking it in his teeth, and then the bone would squeak, and he would look really surprised and drop it on the floor. Then he'd start all over again, until he wore himself out. Hannah spent ages curled up next to his cushion just watching him sleep. He was the most gorgeous thing she had ever seen.

Oscar didn't spend that much of his

sleep time actually *on* his cushion. As soon as he'd finished exploring, he would wander back to wherever Hannah was and collapse on her – he particularly liked her feet, draping himself over them like a spotty, saggy little beanbag and falling fast asleep.

Hannah was worried that the first night was going to be really difficult. How could they leave Oscar all on his own downstairs? But Mum had been really firm from the beginning that Oscar was not allowed in her room. Mum said he would soon be far too big to sleep on her bed, even though he was tiny now. And there were lots of things upstairs that she didn't want chewed.

Lisa had told them about a special technique to get Oscar used to being left alone in the kitchen, and Hannah practised it with him that afternoon. Mum took Zak out for a walk to get him out of the way, and Dad and Hannah pottered about in the kitchen, with Oscar watching them. Then they went out, shutting the door.

"Can we go back in yet?" Hannah asked. "Dad, come on, Lisa said to go back before he gets upset! Remember, you're going to read the paper and pretend you aren't watching him."

Dad nodded and opened the kitchen door. Hannah glanced over at Oscar. He was looking puzzled and a little worried. She looked away again and went to tidy up some cups from the draining board. Then she nudged Dad. "Time to go again!"

They kept popping in and out, making sure that they always got back before Oscar cried. Eventually, he got bored watching and went to sleep.

"Lisa was right," Hannah whispered. "I hope it works tonight."

At bedtime, she took Oscar out for one last wee in the garden, and made sure there was some newspaper down in the corner of the kitchen for the night. Then she closed the door behind her, and looked hopefully at Mum and Dad.

"Lisa said he'd be sure that we're just on the other side of the door," Hannah said. "And he must be worn out from all the playing we've done." But as she pressed her ear to the door, she couldn't help feeling a little doubtful. There was no whining. Just a little tappity-tap of claws on tiles and a snuffling noise. Hannah held her breath.

On the other side of the door, Oscar sniffed thoughtfully, wondering if Hannah would come back in soon. Maybe with some more of those good meaty biscuits? He yawned and padded back to his cushion. He clambered up and flumped on top of his toy bone. It squeaked, and he gave it a half-hearted chew. Perhaps if he went to sleep, it would be food time when he woke up...

Oscar curled up and closed his eyes – and out in the hall, Hannah grinned at her mum and dad. There was a little growly snore coming from behind the kitchen door. It had worked!

Chapter Four

Oscar soon settled into Hannah's house. He loved Hannah and they spent ages playing, Oscar frisking about as she rolled his ball or threw his squeaky bone. After the first couple of days, once Oscar was allowed out of the kitchen, Hannah discovered that he loved to curl up on the sofa with her while she read or watched TV.

Mum wasn't sure about this at first. "When he gets to his full size, he'll take up half the sofa just by himself," she complained. But she gave in eventually, when Oscar sat on her feet while she was watching her favourite TV programme after she'd put Zak to bed. He sat there staring up at her lovingly, and Mum couldn't resist. She sighed and patted the sofa, and Oscar scrambled and wriggled his way up. Then he lay there next to Mum with his head in her lap, slowly thumping his tail on the cushions.

Oscar's only problem was Zak. It wasn't that Zak didn't like him – the little boy adored him and wanted to be with him all the time. He just wouldn't leave the puppy alone. Zak wanted to cuddle Oscar on his cushion. He wanted to snuggle up with him on the sofa. He even wanted to eat his food out of a bowl like Oscar's.

A week after Oscar came home with them, Hannah was up in her room learning her lines for the play when she heard a strange noise on the stairs. A whimpering noise, mixed with bumps, and panting. That was Oscar whimpering – and it sounded like Zak was with him! She flung down her script and dashed out of her bedroom. As she'd suspected, Zak was halfway up the stairs, with Oscar dangling from his arms, looking panicked.

"Want Ossa in my bed!" Zak wailed, when he saw Hannah coming down the stairs looking cross.

"You know we aren't allowed!" Hannah told him furiously. Why did Zak always think he could get away with everything? It wasn't as if she wouldn't like Oscar in *her* bed! Oscar wriggled and whimpered again, and Hannah stretched out her arms to him.

But Zak wouldn't let go. "My dog!" he whined.

"Zak! You're making him sad, stop it. Give him to me!" Hannah was trying not to shout and upset Oscar, but it was hard when she really wanted to yell at Zak.

"Don't want to!"

"Now!" Hannah hissed.

"No!" Zak burst into tears as Oscar finally wriggled out of his grip and scrambled into Hannah's arms.

"Hannah! What are you doing with Oscar – you know he's not allowed upstairs!" Mum had come out into the hallway, and she was glaring at Hannah.

"But I wasn't...!" Hannah gasped.

"And what did you do to upset Zak?" Mum gave her an accusing look as she picked Zak up. He was really howling.

Hannah shook her head in amazement. It was so unfair. Sometimes she just didn't know how Zak managed it. He *never* got into trouble.

After she'd caught Zak taking Oscar upstairs, Hannah made a real effort to keep an eye on her little brother and make sure he wasn't bothering Oscar too much. She was glad when he had had all his vaccinations, and she and Dad could take him out for long walks. Oscar loved it, especially when they took him to the woods. He even loved splashing in the stream, despite the December cold.

One Sunday, Hannah finally persuaded Mum and Dad to let her and Lucy take Oscar for a walk on their own, now that Oscar was used to being on the lead. They agreed the girls could go as long as they borrowed Hannah's mum's mobile, and promised to be back in half an hour.

"We haven't really got time to go all the way to the woods. Shall we go to the park?" Lucy suggested.

Hannah looked thoughtful. "Oh, I know, let's go and show Oscar the horses in the field down past school! Dalmatians used to be carriage dogs, who ran alongside coaches hundreds of years ago. They're supposed to love horses, and I don't think Oscar's ever seen any. Shall I nip back and tell Mum that's where we're going?"

Lucy nodded eagerly, and smiled with pride when Hannah passed her Oscar's lead.

Oscar gazed up at the new girl with interest. She wasn't like Hannah, but she was nice. He then looked hopefully towards the house, waiting for Hannah to come back. When she came running down the path, he yapped happily and danced round her feet.

"He really loves you," Lucy sighed. "You're so lucky!"

"I know." Hannah nodded. "I love you, too, Oscar," she told him, rubbing his ears.

Lucy looked back at the house. "Oh, Zak's waving to us. He looks a bit sad; I bet he wishes he could come too."

Hannah groaned. "He's being such a nightmare at the moment! He won't leave Oscar alone, and Mum keeps making excuses for him. Yesterday he decided he wanted to feed Oscar, and he poured a whole bag of the special dog treats into his bowl, so of course Oscar ate them!" She sighed. "And you know what Mum said? That I should have made sure I put the treats away in the cupboard."

Lucy giggled. "Sometimes I'm glad I'm the youngest!"

The horses the girls were going to see belonged to a riding school, and there were usually a few of them out in one of the fields. At the moment they were wrapped up in rugs and not out for the whole day, but Hannah was pretty sure there would be something for Oscar to see.

Oscar trotted along happily, enjoying the interesting smells and listening to the girls chatting.

"Oh, look, they *are* out!" Hannah said, quickening her pace. "Come on, Oscar." They hurried up to the field to look at the horses, and Hannah picked Oscar up, resting his front paws on the top of the fence. She could feel his tail wagging against her arms, and it made her giggle.

Oscar gazed across the field at the horses, enchanted by the huge creatures. He'd seen other dogs, but never anything as tall and graceful as these.

At last Hannah sighed. "We should get back, or Mum'll be worried. I promise I'll bring you to see them again, Oscar."

Hannah wished she could take Oscar out for a long walk every day, but now that it was getting closer to Christmas, the school play was taking up lots more time. Mr Byford insisted that everyone had to be word-perfect, and he'd planned some extra rehearsals for the main parts after school. Hannah had to go to all of them, because her big part meant she was in every scene.

Hannah loved being in the play, and so far she was dealing with her nerves really well. But the extra rehearsals made it hard to fit in Oscar's walks. By the time she got home from school it was totally dark – and there was no way Mum would let her out to walk

Oscar in the woods. They had to make do with a quick jog round the park with Dad when he got home. Other than that, it was down to Mum to take Oscar for a walk in the morning. But that meant Mum had to have Oscar and Zak's pushchair, which wasn't very easy. Hannah had also been hoping they could start dog-training classes soon, too, but Mum said that with all the rehearsals, there was no way Hannah could fit in anything else. They would have to wait until after Christmas.

Oscar really missed his walks. It seemed ages since he'd had a proper one, and Hannah hardly seemed to be at home at all. He was sick of watching the door, waiting for Hannah to come home. Why wasn't she back?

He thoughtfully
sniffed the shoe
rack in the
hallway and
tugged at a
trailing pink
shoelace.
One of Mum's
trainers fell down, and he
nudged it with his nose. This was fun!
He growled at it, pretending it was
something to chase, and then held it
down with his front paws and started
to gnaw at the laces.

Just then, Mum came down the
stairs. "Oscar, no! No chewing! Bad
dog!" She snatched the trainer back
and shooed him into the kitchen.

Oscar slumped down on his cushion

and licked his nose sadly. He didn't really understand what he'd done wrong. He wanted to go out and have a lovely long run with Hannah. She was still Oscar's favourite person, but she was never there. Why didn't she want to spend time with him any more? He felt bored and grumpy, and that made him want to chew things. He didn't know he wasn't allowed to chew shoes…

He was still looking miserable when Hannah got home at last. She sat down by his cushion to stroke him. "Mum told me about her shoe. I'm sorry she was cross with you, Oscar. You were just bored, weren't you, poor baby." Hannah sighed. "It isn't long till the play now. After that we'll go on lots more walks, I promise."

Chapter Five

Oscar sat on the back of the sofa and stared out of the window, watching for Hannah in the gathering dark. He missed her. It seemed so long since she'd left the house for school that morning. She had taken him out in the garden and they'd played with his jingly ball, which had been fun. But then Hannah's mum had called her in.

Since then he'd only had a quick walk round the park at lunchtime, with Zak trying to hold his lead, and pulling him backwards and forwards.

"Ossa!"

It was Zak again, running into the living room. Oscar whipped his head round and overbalanced. He slid down between the sofa and the window, yelping with fright, although he wasn't really hurt, only surprised.

Zak clambered on to the sofa and hung perilously over the back, looking for Oscar.

Oscar whimpered miserably. He wanted to be left alone until Hannah came back. He started to creep along behind the sofa, meaning to nip out of the living-room door. Hannah's mum was preparing dinner in the kitchen, so she could let him out into the garden, and then he'd be safely away from Zak fussing him and pulling at his ears.

But Zak could move surprisingly fast. He wriggled down from the back of the sofa, and trotted round to meet Oscar as he emerged from behind it.

"Ossa!" The little boy flung his arms around the puppy's neck, squeezing him lovingly.

Oscar moaned. Zak was cuddling him far too tightly, and it hurt. He tried to pull back out of Zak's arms, but that only made Zak hold him tighter. Oscar wriggled and struggled, and Zak giggled, thinking it was all just a funny game.

Oscar was starting to feel desperate. He wanted to snap, but he knew he shouldn't. Instead, he growled. A low *Rrrrrrrrrrr!* deep in his chest, his lips drawing back from his teeth in a snarl.

Zak let go of Oscar, stumbling away, his eyes wide with fright.

Oscar shot out into the hallway, looking for a place to hide in case Zak followed him. There was a little alcove under the stairs where everyone kept their coats and bags, and Oscar scurried into it, hiding behind Hannah's ballet bag. His heart was racing and he felt grumpy and scared at the same time. He hadn't wanted to upset the little boy, but why wouldn't Zak just leave him alone?

His ears pricked up as he heard Hannah coming up the front path, followed by her dad, who'd gone to pick her up from the rehearsal. He longed to leap out and run to her – but Zak might grab him again. Better to stay hidden. He crouched down behind the bag, still shivering.

"Oscar?" Hannah sounded surprised. Usually he was there, dancing around her as soon as she came in the door, but today he was nowhere to be seen.

"I wonder if he's got shut in somewhere," Dad suggested, as Hannah went to put her school bag away under the stairs.

As soon as he saw her, Oscar wriggled out on his tummy, making a little whining noise.

"Oh! He's here! Oscar, what's the matter? Dad, he's shaking." Hannah knelt down to cuddle him, and Oscar snuggled against her gratefully.

"Ossa growled," a small voice said behind Hannah, and she turned round to find Zak standing in the living-room doorway, looking half-guilty, half-scared.

Dad frowned. "What happened, Zak?" he asked.

Mum rushed out into the hall. "Oh no! What's the matter? I was just putting the pasta on and I couldn't hear anything over the sound of the kettle."

"Zak's been bothering Oscar again, I bet!" Hannah burst out. She had felt Oscar tense up as soon as Zak appeared.

"Don't always blame Zak, Hannah. He's only little," Mum said gently.

Hannah sighed.

"Zak, were you chasing Oscar?" Dad asked, looking into Zak's eyes.

Zak wriggled away from him. "No. Jus' stroking."

"You have to be gentle, Zak," Dad explained. "He's only a puppy."

Hannah glared at Zak. He'd got away with it, again! It just wasn't fair! As she cuddled Oscar closer she could feel how upset he was. She only wished she could have been there to protect him.

"I have to make some wings as part of my costume," Hannah told everyone at the dinner table later on. "Mr Byford's going to give me some tissue paper to bring home." She smiled to herself, but it wasn't because of her excitement about her beautiful angel costume. Under the table, a small, warm muzzle was resting lovingly on her foot. Hannah lifted a piece of meat on her fork, and "accidentally" dropped it down the side of her chair. Oscar deserved a treat. A little black and white blur raced to snap it up.

"What else are you wearing, do you know?" Mum asked.

"A gold tunic thing and a halo," Hannah told her. "Mrs Garner's making the halo, she's the lady who comes in to help with art. She's brilliant at making things."

"Sounds good." Dad smiled. "I'm really looking forward to seeing this show next week. We've heard so much about it, I feel like I could join in!"

Hannah grinned. She had gone on about the play a bit, she supposed.

She brought home all the bits for the wings that Friday. They were quite complicated to make, and Dad had to help her over the weekend. Hannah cut out all the tissue paper feathers, and Dad made her a wire frame to stick them on, and helped her tie ribbons on to fasten the wings around her shoulders. They worked on them for two whole evenings, dabbing on gold paint here and there, and making them look really special.

So it was a total disaster when

Hannah came home from school on Monday, the day before the dress rehearsal, and found her wings lying on the living-room floor, with half the feathers ripped off.

"Mum!" Hannah called out, horrified. Mum rushed in from the hallway, where she'd been taking off Zak's coat.

"What is it?"

"Why weren't you watching him?" Hannah wailed. "How could you let him tear them up like that? I hate you, Zak!" she added angrily, as she saw Zak peeping round the door.

"Oh, Hannah, I don't think this was Zak," Mum said, shaking her head. "And don't say that, please. It's mean."

Hannah blinked. "Who was it then?"

"Oscar! Look, they're all chewed. I'm sorry, we shouldn't have left them to dry on that low shelf, but I just didn't think about it." She sighed. "We need to be a bit more careful." She looked down at Oscar, who'd just emerged from behind the sofa. "No, Oscar! Look at this mess!"

"It wasn't Oscar," Hannah said stubbornly, sweeping him up in her arms. But she could see the white tissue paper sticking out of the corner of his mouth, and she knew that Mum was right. Cuddling Oscar tight, she marched out of the living room. There was no way she was saying sorry to Zak.

Dad had helped Hannah remake her wings in time for the dress rehearsal, but they weren't quite as good as they'd been before. Hannah wriggled her shoulders nervously, fussing with the ribbons that held the wings on. She couldn't believe it was the night of the performance at last.

"Can you see them?" Lucy asked, as Hannah peeped round the side of the curtain.

Hannah shook her head. "No. Oh, but your mum and dad are over there!" She frowned as she stared around the hall again. "They're going to have to sit at the back," she murmured. "It's really filling up."

Mum had promised Hannah that she and Dad would be there in good time — they were going to leave Zak with Gran. *So where were they?*

Somebody giggled loudly behind Hannah, making her jump. Everyone was chatting excitedly backstage. They'd brought a packed tea to school, so they could fit in one last run-through before that night's performance. The nerves had been building ever since the bell went for the end of school. Hannah glanced down at the little photo in her hand, a favourite one of Oscar that she'd glued on to card to keep in her school bag. She was feeling a bit jittery about her part, and looking at Oscar's gorgeous face made her feel better.

There was a little flurry at the hall doors, and Hannah's eyes widened. There was Gran! She seemed to be explaining something to Mrs Garner, who was taking the tickets.

But Gran was supposed to be babysitting Zak. Hannah wished she could go and ask Gran what was going on. But she had her costume on ready, and the play was due to start in a few minutes. Hannah stroked Oscar's photo with one finger, her tummy twisting. Why hadn't Mum and Dad come?

Chapter Six

Oscar padded into the hallway, and went to sniff at the front door. Then he sat down for a couple of minutes, before trailing back into the kitchen for a drink from his water bowl.

Where was everyone? Hannah's mum had taken Zak out as usual, and come back on her own to make a cup of tea. But then the phone had rung, startling Oscar out of a sleep. He'd got up from his cushion, feeling sure it was close to food time, and hoping that if he stood next to Hannah's mum and wagged his tail she might feed him.

But she had crashed the phone down so fast it fell out of its holder – and she hadn't even bothered to pick it up again! And then she ran out of the kitchen, so fast that she fell over Oscar. She didn't stop to say sorry, or stroke him, or even tell him off for being in her way. She simply dashed out of the house, without even a coat, and drove off in the car.

She still hadn't come back. Hannah should have been home from school by now, Oscar was sure. And Zak? Surely he should be home now, too?

It felt close to the time that their dad should be back from work as well. Oscar didn't like being left on his own for so long, and he was getting really hungry now. He pattered up the hallway again, his tail hanging low, and then suddenly brightened as he heard footsteps.

Slow, frightened footsteps, not Hannah's usual happy run. He backed away from the door, feeling anxious.

The door opened and Gran came in, followed by Hannah, her angel wings trailing from her hand.

Hannah looked upset, and even though she hugged him, she felt different. She was holding him so tight and he could feel her heart thudding a fast, anxious beat. Oscar nuzzled her worriedly, wondering what was wrong.

"Oh, Oscar, didn't Mum feed you?"
Hannah held him in front of her,
looking into his eyes. "Poor Oscar, you
must be starving. Come on." Hannah
went to get his special dog biscuits.

Oscar waited by his bowl gratefully,
but he didn't feel as hungry as he had
before. He knew that something was
wrong, and he hated seeing Hannah

so unhappy. It made him feel jittery and nervous, and somehow all wrong.

After he'd eaten, he went to sit on the sofa between Hannah and Gran. They had the television on, but they weren't really paying attention to it. It got later and later, and Oscar finally fell asleep on the sofa, curled up against Hannah.

Oscar woke as he heard a car door slam, and he barked sharply to wake Hannah and Gran, who were dozing too. It felt very late.

"Dad!" Hannah ran into the hallway. "What happened? Is Zak OK? Where is he? Where's Mum?"

Dad looked exhausted. "Gran told you he fell off the climbing frame at nursery?"

Hannah nodded. Gran had broken the news after the play.

"He hit his head. Six stitches, would you believe? He's got to stay at the hospital tonight because it was a head injury, and your mum's staying with him." He sat down wearily on the stairs to take off his shoes. "Hannah, sweetheart, I'm so sorry we missed your play. I was really looking forward to it. We didn't know how seriously Zak had been hurt. Mum got a call saying he'd gone to hospital in an ambulance."

Hannah sucked in a breath. That made it sound really serious. "Will he be OK?" she asked again, worriedly.

"They think he'll be fine." Dad was trying to sound reassuring, but he mostly just sounded tired. "Come on.

Let's have some hot chocolate and all go to bed."

Gran stayed the night, and breakfast the next morning was strange with her there, but no Mum and Zak. She dropped Hannah at school, but Dad promised that Mum and Zak would be home from the hospital later that day.

Mum met Hannah from school, but without Zak. She grabbed Hannah in a massive hug.

"Where's Zak? He isn't still in hospital, is he?" Hannah looked up at Mum anxiously.

Mum shook her head. "It's all right, sweetie, he's at home with Gran.

He's miserable, but in a couple of days he'll be fine – he'll probably have a scar, though. Hannah, I've been to see Mrs James in the office, and she said we can get a copy of the DVD of the play. I'm just so sorry we weren't there for the real thing. Did it go all right? Did you enjoy it?"

Hannah nodded. It felt mean to say that actually, she hadn't enjoyed the play all that much, because she'd known something must be wrong. "I remembered all my words."

Mum hugged her again, and Hannah was pretty sure that her mum knew what she wasn't saying. "You couldn't help it, Mum. It's OK, honest."

Her mum sighed. "I still can't help feeling we let you down."

"I really didn't mind." Hannah nodded firmly. Deep inside, she did wish that they'd been there, of course. But when they got home and she saw Zak lying on the sofa, with a huge bandage on his head, she couldn't feel annoyed with him at all. She sat next to Zak all evening, letting him watch the racing car programme she couldn't stand, and stroking Oscar's ears with him.

At least now the play was over and the Christmas holidays had started, Hannah would have loads more time to spend with Oscar. She wanted to make sure his first Christmas was extra special. She was planning lots of lovely long walks, perhaps with Lucy too, and plenty of afternoons curled up on the sofa watching all the good films that were on over the holidays. She was even planning to show Oscar *101 Dalmatians* for the first time!

What made it even more thrilling was that it had snowed. The very first morning of the holidays, Hannah had woken up to find a light powdering over the street, as though someone had shaken icing sugar over a cake. It had snowed again that night, just a little more, and the weather forecasters were promising a white Christmas.

Oscar loved it, although he wasn't sure about getting chilly wet paws. He liked to watch the snow too, sitting on the back of the sofa with his nose pressed up against the window, snapping his teeth at the flakes twirling down outside.

In all the excitement, Hannah had forgotten that her aunt was coming to stay for Christmas. She lived in Scotland, so she and Zak didn't get to see her very often, and this was the first time she'd met Oscar.

Unfortunately, Auntie Jess wasn't very keen on dogs. She didn't want

Oscar in the living room all the time, and she kept brushing at her clothes, as though Oscar's hair had got on them. She was always very smartly dressed, and she wore a lot of black, so the white hairs really showed up. Hannah took Oscar out in the garden for an extra good grooming session, but it didn't seem to make any difference.

Oscar had never met anyone who didn't like him before. When Auntie Jess first arrived, he tried to say hello in his normal way, wagging his tail and nuzzling at her legs, and looking up at her with his funny Dalmatian smile. But she stepped back nervously.

"Oh! Why is it showing its teeth like that? Does it bite?" Auntie Jess looked horrified.

"Of course not!" Hannah cried. "He's just being friendly. And he's called Oscar."

"Put him in the kitchen, Hannah," Mum said quickly. Hannah scowled, but did as she was told. Oscar hadn't done anything wrong! She hoped Auntie Jess would get used to him.

Oscar was confused. The house was full of strange things, like that big flashy tree that wobbled and jingled. And that strange lady kept pushing him away, and Hannah seemed to be with her all the time. So he stayed on his own in the kitchen on his cushion, feeling miserable.

Hannah did her best to cheer him up, and she did manage to take Oscar for a couple of proper walks, but Mum kept saying that Auntie Jess wasn't here for long, and it was rude to go off without her. Hannah thought about suggesting that Auntie Jess came too, but she didn't think that would go down very well. She did love Auntie Jess — she just wished that her aunt liked dogs too.

Oscar curled up on his cushion, feeling lonely. He tucked his nose under his tail, and imagined a long run in the woods, with Hannah laughing and jumping beside him. She'd played with him in the garden that morning, but it just wasn't the same. And now they'd all gone out. Hannah had promised they would be back soon, but they had been gone for ages. Oscar turned round grumpily. He was sick of his cushion, and the kitchen.

Perhaps now would be a good time to go and look at that strange tree again. He trotted into the living room, and gazed up at it. He didn't trust it, and he wasn't sure why it was in his house.

Sniffing suspiciously, Oscar walked all round the tree, which was surrounded by rustly parcels. The twirly ribbon on one of them caught around his paw, and he shook it. It sprang back. Oscar patted the ribbon with his paw. It was trying to escape!

He seized the parcel in his teeth, shaking it to and fro fiercely – he loved the feel of the paper tearing. Then he settled down happily to chew the long, pink woolly thing that was inside.

When Hannah, Zak and their parents and Auntie Jess walked in from their Christmas shopping trip a little while later, Oscar was fast asleep on the living-room floor. He was surrounded by shreds of silver wrapping paper and twirly ribbon, and the ruins of the pretty, fluffy pink scarf that had been Auntie Jess's Christmas present for Hannah.

"Oh! Look what that naughty dog's done!" Auntie Jess cried. "You really need to get him to behave. He's ruined Hannah's present!"

Oscar woke up and slunk guiltily over to Hannah, trailing pink ribbons.

"Bad dog, Oscar!" Mum said crossly.

"You aren't!" Hannah whispered, cuddling him. She looked up at Mum. "It isn't really his fault. We left him alone all day. I know he was naughty, but it's because he's bored!" Then she added very quietly, "And I didn't like that scarf anyway, Oscar..."

Chapter Seven

Everyone woke early on Christmas Day. Hannah and Zak were desperate to open their stockings, and Mum and Dad had to start cooking the Christmas lunch. Gran was coming, and their other grandma and grandad, and Uncle Mark and his family – Hannah and Zak's three little cousins. Dad had bought an enormous turkey.

Oscar was sitting by the oven looking hopeful – it smelled so good!

Hannah was really looking forward to seeing her cousins again, but she was worried about Oscar. Jamie, Tara and Phoebe were all quite young – Phoebe was only two like Zak – and they weren't really used to dogs. Hannah had a horrible feeling they would be chasing round trying to hug Oscar all day, and he wasn't going to like it.

Luckily, Oscar loved his Christmas present from her, a really big chewy bone, and that distracted him for a little while, even when Uncle Mark and all the children arrived. But then they spotted Oscar lying on his cushion.

"Hello, doggie!" Phoebe squealed.

"Oooohh!" Tara cried excitedly.

"Can I play with him?" Tara didn't even wait for an answer, she ran straight at Oscar, and sat down on his cushion next to him.

Oscar jumped back in horrified surprise. One minute he'd been happily chewing his lovely new bone, and the next minute somebody was trying to grab it off him! He looked up at Hannah pleadingly, begging her to rescue him.

"Tara, Oscar's cushion is his special place," Hannah started to explain. "He doesn't like other people sitting on it."

Tara's face went sulky. "Don't boss me about!" she told Hannah crossly.

"I'm not," Hannah sighed. She gave Oscar a gentle pat, and he clambered off his cushion and scuttled out into the hallway.

Everywhere Oscar went that morning Auntie Jess kept glancing nervously at him, or one of the cousins was grabbing at him. And then Uncle Mark accidentally kicked him when he was sitting under the table hoping for a treat during Christmas lunch. Oscar dashed out from under the table with a howl, and Hannah scooped him up and cuddled him.

"You're having a bad day, aren't you, Oscar?" she murmured. "Poor sweetie. Mum, can I give Oscar a little bit of turkey? Please? Just to cheer him up?"

Mum looked doubtful, but then she said, "Oh, I suppose as a Christmas treat. But in his food bowl in the kitchen, Hannah, so he doesn't think he's being fed from the table."

Hannah nodded and tried not to look guilty. She quite often slipped Oscar bits of food under the table. She knew she shouldn't, but he had such good eyes for begging with.

The turkey was the best bit of the day for Oscar. It was delicious, and he forgot about the noisy, grabby children while he was wolfing it down. But as soon as the Christmas lunch was finished, he saw Jamie slipping down from his chair and reaching out to stroke him. Oscar made a dash for it out of the living room, where Mum and Dad had set up a folding table for lunch.

Out in the hallway he made for his hiding place under the stairs, wriggling right to the back under a pile of coats.

"Where's your dog gone?" Jamie asked Hannah.

Hannah crossed her fingers behind her back. "I don't know," she told him. She didn't actually; it wasn't a total lie. But she very much suspected he was hiding under the stairs.

Dad called Jamie to come back into the living room, telling everyone that a really good film was about to start, and the little boy ran off. Hannah gave a relieved sigh. If she helped Mum finish off clearing the table and everyone else was watching the film, perhaps she could sneak off and give Oscar a cuddle on his own – without any cousins or little brothers wanting to join in.

Oscar lay there in the dark, remembering the taste of the turkey, and wishing Hannah was there. But he didn't dare come out of his hiding place to find her.

Hannah carried the last of the empty pudding bowls into the kitchen, and piled them up next to all the other plates. "I'm just going to check on Oscar," she told her mum.

"Oh yes," Mum said. "He's not really enjoying all these people, is he? Do you want to stay in here with him for a bit? I don't think he'll want to go in the living room."

"Won't Auntie Jess and Granny and Gran and everyone think I'm being rude?" Hannah asked.

Mum laughed. "I think they're all going to fall asleep watching this film, Hannah, everyone's so full of food. It'll be fine."

"Thanks, Mum." Hannah hugged her.

Her mum hugged her back, but then let go quickly. "Oh no! What's Zak screaming about?" And she hurried off to the living room to sort it out.

Hannah sighed. Zak again, just when she'd been having a nice moment with Mum. She padded out into the hallway, spotting Mum cuddling a still-wailing Zak. Jamie and Tara were moaning that they couldn't hear the film, and Phoebe looked like she might join in the howling.

Hannah squeezed herself into the alcove under the stairs, and giggled as a chilly little nose dabbed at her hand. "You've got the right idea, Oscar," she murmured. "It's a nightmare out there!"

Oscar nuzzled her gratefully, feeling sure that she would protect him from the other children. He climbed into her lap and huffed out a satisfied little yawn. He was safe now Hannah was with him.

Hannah stroked him thoughtfully. "It's a bit squished for me under here, Oscar." She sighed. "But I really don't want to go and watch that film with all the others." She could still hear Zak moaning, and Mum was sounding as though she was losing patience. Then Hannah brightened, a smile curving her lips. "Let's go for a walk, Oscar! A special Christmas walk."

Oscar scrambled down from her lap, his tail wagging. He knew what walk meant, and he definitely approved of the idea.

"Let's go and ask Mum." Hannah hauled herself out of the gap under the stairs.

But when she peeped round the living-room door, with Oscar peeping round her legs in turn, Zak's moans had progressed into a full-blown wobbly. Mum and Dad strode past her

– Dad carrying Zak, and Mum looking embarrassed and cross. It wasn't the time to go asking about walks.

But Oscar was looking up at her so hopefully. Hannah frowned. "I know. We'll leave a note for Mum on the kitchen table. I'm sure it'll be OK."

She fetched Oscar's lead, and wrapped herself in her warmest things, putting on an extra pair of socks before stepping into her wellies. The snow was quite thick out there.

The living-room door was part open and she could see Gran was asleep on the sofa, with little Phoebe asleep on her. Hannah didn't want to wake them, or disturb the others watching the film. She wrote a quick note, promising to be back soon, and left it on the kitchen table. With a sudden excited smile, she took a couple of carrots from the vegetable basket. Then she and Oscar slipped quietly out of the front door.

A few minutes later, Mum came down after settling Zak for a sleep. She fetched the mince pies out of the living room, just in case Oscar tried to nibble them, and put down the plate on the kitchen table. Right on top of Hannah's note.

Chapter Eight

Oscar padded happily through the crisp snow, his paws crunching at every step. It felt good and he wanted to run. He looked up hopefully at Hannah. She laughed, and they raced down the road.

"I've got some carrots," Hannah told Oscar, when they stopped, panting, the cold air burning their throats. "Shall we go and see the horses?"

They walked past Hannah's school, where the playground was a sheet of snow, without a single footprint. At last, they reached the riding school fields. The horses were standing clustered together, looking rather mournful.

"The carrots will cheer them up," Hannah told Oscar. As they reached the fence, she boosted Oscar up so that he had his paws on the top rail, and she rested his bottom against her. "Ooh, Oscar, I'm not sure how long I can do this," she told him. "You're definitely getting heavier!"

She held the carrots out invitingly, and the horses came trotting over.

Oscar wagged his tail delightedly and stretched out his nose to nuzzle at the horses as they gobbled the carrots.

"Mind they don't accidentally nibble you too," Hannah warned him, laughing as she pulled him away. They watched happily as the horses nosed around, looking for more carrots. Finally, they gave up and wandered off.

Hannah sighed. "I suppose we should go home. It's starting to snow again, look!"

Oscar gazed up at her. He could tell from her tone that she didn't really want to, and he wagged his tail hopefully.

"I suppose we could stay out a little longer," Hannah said slowly. "It isn't getting dark yet, and I shouldn't think anyone will have missed us." She sighed again and hugged Oscar close, feeling suddenly lonely.

But her sad mood was quickly broken as Oscar licked her face lavishly, making her splutter and giggle. "OK. Let's go to the woods, shall we? We can walk down to the stream. It might even be frozen!"

They tramped along the snowy path, Hannah admiring the layer of crystal snow decorating the branches as they drew closer to the woods. It had drifted deeply under the trees, and Hannah and Oscar ran along kicking up the snow, Oscar barking happily. His barks echoed around the empty woodland, and Hannah chased him in and out of the dark trees.

Oscar felt better than he had in ages. All the grumpiness had gone. He shook his ears and barked, then barked again as a load of snow fell down from a branch with a shivery thump.

At last, they settled down for a rest on a fallen tree by the edge of the stream. It was so beautiful – the stream was just starting to ice over at the edges. Hannah sighed happily. This was much better than sitting in the stuffy house. But they should probably go back soon, or it would be getting dark. She looked up at the sky and realized with a sharp shock that the sun was out again, but it was low in the sky, and the shadows had grown longer and darker. They must have been out longer than she had thought. She sprang up anxiously. "We need to go home, Oscar. It's late."

Oscar looked up at her, and wagged his tail uncertainly. Hannah sounded upset.

She looked around, her eyes wide. "Oscar, which way did we come? I can only see our footsteps just here by the fallen tree, the snow's covered the rest of them." She shook herself angrily. "Oh, this is stupid, we can't be lost." She walked around the tree trunk, looking carefully at the little paths leading off between the trees.

Which one had they come along? Panic was growing inside her, and her heart was racing. Every time she looked up, the sky was a deeper shade of eerie night-time blue.

"It's this one, I think," she muttered uncertainly. "Come on, Oscar." She didn't notice Oscar looking back as they set off down the path. He sniffed at the tree trunks thoughtfully as they walked. Why were they going this way?

"This isn't right," Hannah said anxiously, after a few minutes. "We ought to be coming out of the trees by now. We'll have to go back." She led Oscar down the path again, stumbling over the snow in the gathering dark. Back at the clearing by the stream, Hannah sat down again, for her legs were shaking. She had to admit that she didn't know the way.

They were lost.

Oscar looked up at Hannah, confused. She was crying, and he didn't know why. He leaned his head against her leg lovingly, and she looked down and patted him.

"I'm scared, Oscar," she murmured. "And it's so cold. I just want to go home."

Oscar bounced up, wagging his tail. He knew home, and he could get there. Was that all Hannah wanted? He pulled gently on his lead, and gave a little whine. When she looked up, he barked, telling her to follow.

Hannah blinked. "Home?" she asked. "Can you get us home, Oscar?"

Oscar tugged his lead, and Hannah stumbled after him. The path he chose looked just like all the others to her, but

he seemed so sure. Every so often he would stop to sniff at the bushes, then he'd wag his tail and pull her on.

Hannah looked around doubtfully, but Oscar knew exactly where he was going. He trotted on through the wood, and at last she saw the riding school fields at the end of the pathway.

"Oh, Oscar, you little star!" she murmured, crouching down to give him a hug. "But we have to hurry up and get home." Then her shoulders drooped. "Actually, I suppose it doesn't matter, except that I'm getting really cold, and I bet you are too. I shouldn't think anyone will have noticed we've been gone."

They trudged home, past the school, and turned at last into their road. Oscar pricked up his ears as they came round the corner, and Hannah stopped in surprise. Someone was calling her name. And there it was again. It sounded like Gran.

"Hannah! Hannah!" And that was her dad.

Hannah started walking again, Oscar pulling her down the road. Gran, and Granny and Grandpa, Dad and Uncle Mark, and even Auntie Jess were out in her road, all calling for her.

They *had* missed her then! Her dad looked really worried, and Hannah slowed down a little, realizing that he was probably going to be furious.

"Hannah!" Dad caught sight of her and ran up the road, swinging her into his arms and squeezing her tight. "Where were you? We were so worried, we had no idea where you were!"

"I left a note!" Hannah said,

surprised. "You and Mum were busy with Zak, and Oscar was so miserable… I'm sorry," she added. "I didn't mean to be so late. I got lost in the wood, and Oscar found the way home. He was really clever."

Dad was still holding her as though he thought she might disappear. "We didn't find a note. Oh, Hannah, you should have told us."

"But Zak was screaming…"

"It's OK – we're not cross. We were scared, Hannah. Please promise you'll never go off like that again."

"I won't. Promise." Hannah nodded.

Dad crouched down to make a fuss of Oscar. "He brought Hannah home," he told everyone, as they came up the garden path. "Get inside, Hannah, you must be frozen."

"Oscar brought you back?" Auntie Jess asked in surprise. "But he's still just a puppy! Clever boy, Oscar!" And she reached down and patted him gently.

Hannah beamed – Auntie Jess had never stroked Oscar before.

"Hannah!" Zak came running to hug her, and then he hugged Oscar too.

"We were so worried about you!" Mum told her.

"Sorry," Hannah whispered, but she was watching Zak and Oscar worriedly. Then she realized that Oscar didn't have his ears laid back, and he was thumping his tail on the hall floor.

"Wow!" Mum murmured. "Oscar's not being nervous around Zak." She looked at Oscar thoughtfully. "I suppose he's just had a really good long walk. You've exercised some of his nerves away, Hannah." Then she frowned as Zak tried to pick Oscar up. "No, Zak. You can stroke Oscar, but you don't pull him around, OK."

Hannah looked at Mum in amazement, as she gently pulled Zak away. "Come on, Oscar's tired and he

123

wants to go and lie on his cushion now. You play with your new aeroplane. Granny and Grandpa want to see it." Zak made a face, but he did as he was told, and Mum looked over at Hannah. "What is it?"

"You *never* make Zak leave Oscar alone!" Hannah gasped.

Mum sighed. "Well, we probably should have done. Oscar's a patient dog, but Zak needs to be a bit more gentle. We've been letting him get away with stuff because he's only little, but this is important. Sorry, Hannah. I know it's hard being the big sister sometimes."

"Thanks, Mum!" Hannah threw her arms round her. Then she let go, looking thoughtfully through the living-room door at Zak playing with their grandparents. "Oscar is Zak's dog too, though, I suppose. I probably ought to let him join in more." She sighed, and then brightened up. "When we start dog-training, do you think Zak can come too? He might learn to be more gentle with Oscar if he saw everybody at dog-training being really careful with their dogs."

Mum laughed. "We need to get on and book those classes after Christmas. But right now Oscar deserves a bit more turkey, don't you think? Come on, Oscar!"

Hannah nodded, then she put her head round the living-room door. "Zak! Do you want to come and give Oscar some turkey?"

Zak jumped up and took Hannah's hand. They followed Oscar as he trotted eagerly into the kitchen, and watched him gobble up the turkey. He pushed the bowl round the floor, licking round the sides, making sure he hadn't missed any. Then he sighed happily, licked Hannah's foot and slumped down on his cushion.

Hannah giggled, and Zak giggled too, looking up at his big sister. Oscar was stretched out on his cushion with his nose in one corner and his back paws almost touching the other. He thumped his tail just a little as he heard them laugh. Then he sighed and wriggled himself back into a ball – worn out, and full, and very, very happy to be home.

Coming soon:

Lucy the Poorly Puppy